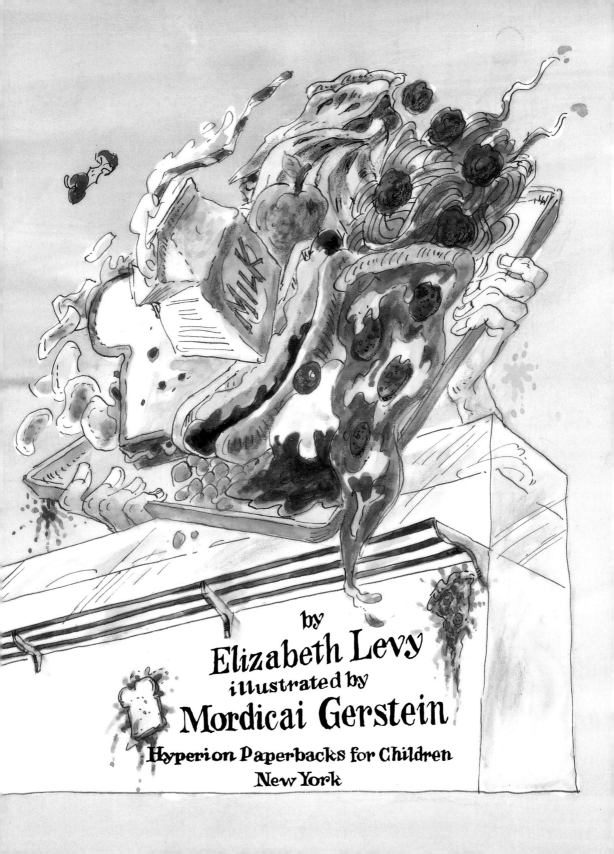

by
Elizabeth Levy
illustrated by
Mordicai Gerstein

Hyperion Paperbacks for Children
New York

To Prune Whip, Salami, and Nan, who ate it all with
me. To Risa, who came up with the idea. And to
Lauri, who made it so much better.
—E.L.

This one is for you, Risa. With love, Daddy.
—M.G.

Text © 1994 Elizabeth Levy.
Illustrations © 1994 Mordicai Gerstein.
Printed in the United States of America.
For information address Hyperion Books for Children,
114 Fifth Avenue, New York, New York 10011.

First Hyperion Paperback edition: September 1994
1 3 5 7 9 10 8 6 4 2

Library of Congress Cataloging-in-Publication Data
Levy, Elizabeth.
Something queer in the cafeteria / Elizabeth Levy;
illustrated by Mordicai Gerstein
1st Hyperion Paperback ed.
p.   cm.
Summary: Jill and Gwen have never gotten into trouble before,
but suddenly every time they're in the cafeteria,
something goes terribly wrong.
ISBN 0-7868-0001-1 (trade)—0-7868-1000-9 (pbk.)
[1. School lunchrooms, cafeterias, etc.—Fiction.]
I. Gerstein, Mordicai, ill.   II. Title.
PZ7.L5827Snm   1994   [Fic]—dc20   93-31343   CIP   AC

Gwen looked down at the soggy pizza on her tray. The new cafeteria at the Evergreen Avenue School was supposed to have opened in the fall. It had finally opened today. It was the first day of March. The pizza looked like it had been cooked in September.

"May I have a crisp piece?" asked Gwen.

"No!" snapped Ms. Claudia Lensky, the woman in charge of the cafeteria.

"Good old M.C.L.," muttered Jill.

Ms. Lensky hadn't changed during the renovation. She wore the same clunky black shoes with square heels. Her uniform looked as scratchy and as uncomfortable as ever. Little tufts of hair still stuck out around her white cap. And she was definitely as mean as ever. Gwen and Jill called her M.C.L.—aka Mean Cafeteria Lady.

NOTE: AKA MEANS, "ALSO KNOWN AS!"

CLOSE-UP OF M.C.L.'S CLUNKY SHOES

CLOSE-UP OF FLETCHER'S BIG STOMACH

"Gwen, here's a mystery for you," said Jill as they sat down at their table. "How come the food in the new cafeteria is worse than in the old one?" Everybody knew that Gwen loved mysteries. She always tapped her braces whenever something queer was going on. Jill held up her pizza. It drooped as badly as her dog Fletcher's big stomach.

Ms. Lensky walked by as Jill's tomato sauce dripped on the table. "Jill, you're making a mess!" snapped Ms. Lensky. She reached over to wipe off the table and knocked over Risa's milk with her elbow.

Ms. Lensky put her hands on her hips. "Risa! You spilled milk all over our brand-new cafeteria."

Risa bit her lower lip. "Hey," said Gwen, "Risa didn't spill her milk. You did."

Ms. Lensky spun around toward Gwen. A blob of
tomato sauce on Ms. Lensky's towel splattered on Natán.
He dropped his spoon on his plate, and a glob of mashed

potatoes flew onto Emma. She aimed a pea in Clifton's direction that missed him and hit Shauntrece.

"Food fight!" yelled Shauntrece. Mashed potatoes and soggy pizza flew in all directions.

Mrs. Greaton, the principal, blew her whistle. "Who started this?"

MRS. GREATON

Ms. Lensky pointed her finger at Gwen and Jill. Gwen blinked. "Not us!" she said.

"We will have no food fights here—especially not in the new cafeteria," said Mrs. Greaton. "I want both of you to stay after school and help clean up this mess."

"Yes, ma'am," muttered Jill, who had never had to stay after school before. Jill hated being in trouble.

Mr. Liu, Gwen and Jill's homeroom teacher, was very upset when he found out two of his students had started a food fight.

"It's not like you," he said. "I was counting on your help decorating the cake for the cafeteria's official grand-opening party. It's for the mayor and the school board. All your families will be invited."

"What about Fletcher?" asked Risa. "He's part of Jill's family. He's almost part of our class." Fletcher waited for Gwen and Jill outside of school every day. He was practically the class mascot. Mr. Liu smiled. He knew how much the class loved Fletcher.

"Perhaps. If Gwen and Jill stay out of trouble," said Mr. Liu.

"We will," promised Gwen and Jill.

"We want to help decorate the cake," said Gwen.

After school Gwen
and Jill went to the
cafeteria to clean up.
Ms. Lensky was
talking to a man
wearing jeans and
cowboy boots. He
smiled at Gwen and
Jill. Ms. Lensky
frowned at them.
"These girls are
nothing but trouble,"
Ms. Lensky said to the
man. "Gwen and Jill,
you can start by filling
a bucket and washing
the floor."

"I think she's got
us confused with
Cinderella," Gwen
muttered.

MOP
WRINGER

Gwen tried to turn on the water. The knob wouldn't budge. She used her muscles. The knob came off. Water squirted all over her face. "Yikes!" shouted Gwen.

Ms. Lensky whirled around. "Look what you did now!"

The man grabbed the knob and stuck it back on. "No harm done," he said.

"It just came off," said Gwen. Jill handed her a towel.

"By itself?" asked Ms. Lensky sarcastically.

When Gwen and Jill finished cleaning, they went outside. Fletcher was waiting with a red bandanna around his collar. His nose barely showed through the snowdrifts. Everyone was sick of the snow but Fletcher. It reminded him of whipped cream.

FLETCHER

(TAIL WAGGING)

Jill hugged him. "We've had the worst day," she said. Fletcher licked her face.

"At least you got an invitation to our party next week," Gwen told Fletcher. "Our class is decorating the cake. Don't eat anything else. The cafeteria food stinks."

Fletcher licked Gwen's face, too.

The next morning after math class, Mr. Liu showed them his design for a cake in the shape of the cafeteria.

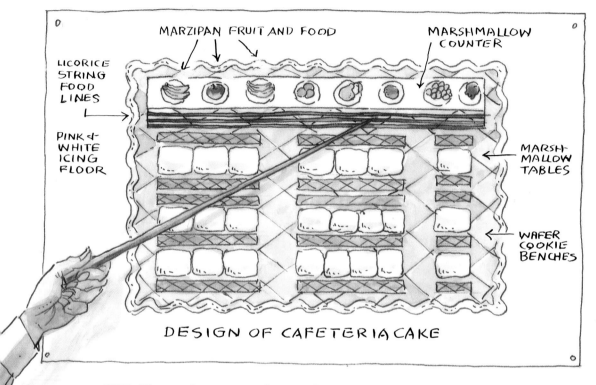

MARZIPAN FRUIT AND FOOD

MARSHMALLOW COUNTER

LICORICE STRING FOOD LINES

PINK & WHITE ICING FLOOR

MARSH-MALLOW TABLES

WAFER COOKIE BENCHES

DESIGN OF CAFETERIA CAKE

"We'll go down to the cafeteria to practice decorating the cake," said Mr. Liu. "We want it to be perfect for next week."

As they walked down the hall, terrible stinking smells wafted out of the cafeteria.

"P.U.," said Luis, holding his nose.

Even Mr. Liu wrinkled his nose.

TOFU IS A CUSTARDY, HIGH-PROTEIN FOOD MADE FROM SOYBEANS. IT CAN BE USED AS A MEAT OR CHEESE SUBSTITUTE AND IS EVEN EATEN SWEETENED AS A DESSERT. IT IS ESPECIALLY POPULAR IN ASIA, WHERE IT ORIGINATED.

As they walked into the kitchen, Ms. Lensky pulled something black and crispy from under the broiler. "They're shriveling up!" she yelled to the same man who had been there the day before.

"You must have overcooked the tofu," said the man.

"Oh, yuck!" said Gwen. "Tofu dogs!"

"You see, the children don't even *like* tofu dogs," he said.

"I've brought my class to practice decorating the cake for the official grand-opening party," said Mr. Liu.

The man in the cowboy boots extended his hand to Mr. Liu. "I'm Charlie Peacock," he said. "My company was in charge of the cafeteria construction. I'm here to make sure that the equipment is being used properly."

The class took turns mixing the sugar and butter for the frosting. When it was Gwen's turn, she rolled up her sleeves.

Suddenly the counter creaked. The bowl started slipping and sliding. The counter collapsed with a great crash. Gwen ended up with frosting all over her.

Mr. Liu reached Gwen first. "What happened?"

Gwen's eyes were wide. "The counter just fell," she said.

"Just fell!" squawked Ms. Lensky. "I bet you kids were sitting on it. As if I didn't have enough problems. The tofu dogs crumble. The pizza droops. Now my counters are falling down!"

"Wait a poky minute," drawled Mr. Peacock. "You know how kids can be. It's not this little girl's fault. It was just an accident."

"An accident or sabotage?" growled Ms. Lensky. "Out! Out!"

Even Mr. Liu was no match for Ms. Lensky on the warpath. "Gwen, why don't you go wash up?" he suggested.

MR. PEACOCK

Jill went into the bathroom with Gwen. Gwen started to tap her braces. Instead of "tap, tap, tap…," it came out "squish, squish, squish." Her braces were full of frosting. "There is definitely something queer going on," she said.

"We get in trouble every time we walk into the cafeteria. Maybe it's jinxed," said Jill.

"Yeah, or haunted by M.C.L.," said Gwen.

"It can't get worse," said Jill.

"Want to bet?" said Gwen.

THE CAFETERIA PANTRY STOCKED WITH INDUSTRIAL-SIZE PEANUT BUTTER & MAYO

That day at lunch, there was nothing but peanut-butter-and-mayonnaise sandwiches. "It *has* gotten worse," admitted Jill. "Peanut-butter-and-mayonnaise should be against the law."

"I like peanut-butter-and-mayonnaise," said George.

"After Gwen's 'accident' in the kitchen, everything I cooked was ruined, and the tofu dogs have disappeared," snapped Ms. Lensky. "Peanut-butter-and-mayonnaise is all I have left. There's Jell-O for dessert."

"The Jell-O is runny," said Risa, staring down at her tray.

"Where's it running?" asked Clifton.

"Anywhere but in my stomach," said Gwen.

Gwen's Jell-O wobbled right off her tray.

"Don't even think about starting another food fight!" yelled Ms. Lensky.

"It fell off my plate," protested Gwen.

"Just wobbled by itself," said Ms. Lensky. "And the knob just came off and the counter just collapsed. I know you're the troublemaker here. You're probably the one who took the tofu dogs."

Gwen glared at her. "I wouldn't touch a tofu dog," said Gwen, "even if it was the last food on earth."

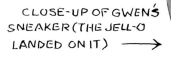

CLOSE-UP OF GWEN'S SNEAKER (THE JELL-O LANDED ON IT) ⟶

"What's going
on, Ms. Lensky?"
asked Mrs.
Greaton.

"These two
pranksters tried to
start another food
fight, and I think
they stole the tofu
dogs. I heard
Gwen say tofu
dogs were yucky,"
said Ms. Lensky.

"Wait one
minute," argued
Jill. "Gwen is not
a thief."

"Gwen and Jill,
I warned you,"
said Mrs. Greaton.
"I'll look into
these pranks. But I
still don't like rude
remarks about the
food. I want you to
stay after school
and write a letter
of apology to Ms.
Lensky."

Gwen and Jill went to detention hall after school. Gwen scribbled, "Dear Cafeteria Lady from the Black Lagoon" on a piece of paper. She showed it to Jill, who giggled.

"No laughing in detention," said Mrs. Greaton.
Gwen sighed. She crumpled up her paper. Gwen and Jill both wrote letters saying they were very sorry to Ms. Lensky. They didn't mean it.

"Where's Fletcher?" asked Jill when they finally got out. "Do you think he got tired of waiting and went home?"

CLOSE-UP OF BANDANNA →

"There he is," said Gwen. A tiny flap of red bandanna was sticking out of a snowdrift. Snow was flying in all directions.

"What's Fletcher doing?" asked Jill. "He never digs so fast."

"Unless there's food," said Gwen.

TOFU DOG

Fletcher lifted his head. He had something in his mouth. He made a face and spit it out.

"A tofu dog!" said Gwen. Fletcher washed his mouth out with snow. The very thought of tofu dogs was just too much.

Jill stared at the snowdrift. "There are hundreds of tofu dogs buried out here."

Gwen tapped her braces. "Look!" she said excitedly, pointing to a square heel print in the snow.

"That heel is from the ugliest shoes in the world. Ms. Lensky's shoes. We can prove we didn't do it. She dumped the tofu dogs out here herself and wanted to blame us. She's the meanest cafeteria lady on the planet earth."

"In the solar system," said Jill.

"In the galaxy," said Gwen.

"In the universe," said Jill.

"And now *she's* in trouble," said Gwen, rubbing her hands together.

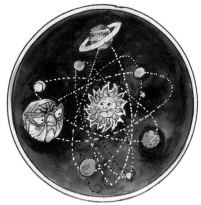

THE SOLAR SYSTEM WITH PLANET M.C.L.

Fletcher was so happy that he rolled over in the snow, right on top of the footprints. "Fletcher's destroying the evidence!" cried Jill. "How will we prove we didn't do it now? The footprints are all smooshed up."

Gwen stared down at the smoothed out snow. She raised her eyes up to the sky. "I don't know how we'll prove Ms. Lensky did it," she said quietly. "But as Fletcher is my witness, we'll never eat tofu dogs again."

On the day of the official party, Gwen and Jill put on their best party dresses. Jill wore a red dress that matched her hair. She even got Fletcher a brand-new bandanna and wrote his name on it with fabric paint.

← CLOSE-UP OF FLETCHER'S BANDANNA

Gwen wore purple, her favorite color. The orthodontist had even changed her braces to purple.

Mr. Liu was pleased that they had gotten dressed up. "I've got aprons for everybody," he said as he took the class to the kitchen to put the final touches on the cake.

Ms. Lensky's hair was sticking out of her cap. "I just know something will go wrong today with those two in the kitchen," she said, looking at Gwen and Jill. "And I'll be blamed."

"We won't let her blame us again," Gwen whispered to Jill.

"Let's get to work, girls and boys," said Mr. Liu. He showed them the huge sheet cake he had baked in the shape of the cafeteria. He handed hairnets to all the kids with long hair, even Clifton. "We don't want any stray hairs in our frosting," said Mr. Liu.

Gwen and Jill went to work untangling the shoestring licorice.

"This is going to be the most excellent cake in the world," said Risa.

"Wait until we get the marshmallows on," said Clifton. "It'll look perfect!"

When the frosting was all spread out and the marshmallows placed just so, Mr. Liu put the cake in the oven to brown the top of the marshmallows.

"There's Mr. Peacock," said Jill.

"He's talking to my mom and Fletcher." Mr. Peacock was wearing a big cowboy hat and a bandanna.

THE MAYOR

"He's nice," said Gwen. "He defended us against M.C.L."

"There's the mayor," said Luis.

"She's about to make her speech," said Mr. Liu. "We should all be in there."

In the middle of the mayor's speech, Gwen sniffed. "I smell something burning," she said. With Fletcher in the lead, the whole class rushed back into the kitchen. Black smoke poured out of the oven. Mr. Peacock was spraying a fire extinguisher into it. The flames sputtered and died.

Mr. Peacock pulled the cake out and dropped it on the floor. "This cake is too hot to handle," he said. It was covered with foam. The marshmallow tables were as black as Fletcher's nose.

"Gross!" said George.

MELTED MARZIPAN

MARSHMALLOW TABLES

FLETCHER'S NOSE

Mr. Liu stared at the mess. "The marshmallows shouldn't have burned. I put the cake in the middle rack, and the oven was only at 250 degrees."

Mr. Peacock turned toward Gwen and Jill with a disappointed look. "Ms. Lensky has been complaining about sabotage, but I didn't believe her. Somebody deliberately ruined that cake. What's that in the oven?" He pulled out a foamy, burned bandanna. "I think this is a clue."

Gwen stared at him. She was the one who usually found clues.

Ms. Lensky looked at Fletcher. "Jill's dog was wearing a bandanna the last time I saw him. Gwen and Jill did it again!"

Everybody stared at Gwen and Jill. Gwen and Jill looked at Fletcher. His bandanna *was* missing!

"I think I'd better talk to the principal," said Mr. Peacock. As he walked out he slipped on the gooey cake frosting. He almost fell down, but he held on to the red bandanna and left a sticky trail behind him.

(MELTED MARSHMALLOW)

"Do something, Gwen," urged Jill. "That was Fletcher's bandanna. We're getting blamed again. This time we could get kicked out of school!"

Gwen tapped her braces. She was stumped. "Somehow Ms. Lensky burned the cake and planted Fletcher's bandanna so we'd be blamed," said Gwen. "I just don't know how to prove it."

"THINK!" demanded Jill.

Ms. Lensky sat down and wept. "The party's ruined. Gwen and Jill, how could you do this? We'll never get another cent to fix all the things that are wrong in the new cafeteria. Mr. Peacock spent over a hundred thousand dollars to build it. Nothing works right."

"Why should things be wrong if they're brand-new?" Gwen asked.

"Stop worrying about that and figure out how to prove Ms. Lensky did it," whispered Jill.

"I am," said Gwen, still tapping.

"Why does she keep doing that?" Ms. Lensky asked Jill. "It's very annoying."

"Gwen always taps her braces when she's detecting. She's a very good detective."

Gwen stared down at the cake on the floor. "I might have made a mistake," she said.

"What? What kind of mistake?" said Jill through gritted teeth. "We're about to be expelled."

"Ms. Lensky," said Gwen. "There's something queer in the cafeteria and I need your help."

"Me?" asked Ms. Lensky. "Why should I help you?"

"Because I'm going to prove Jill and I haven't been messing with your cafeteria. But you have to do me a favor. Step in the cake."

Ms. Lensky glared at her. "Please," pleaded Gwen. "I need your help to solve the mystery—the mystery of why everything's gone wrong in the new cafeteria. Jill and I haven't done the things that we've gotten in trouble for. But somebody has. Please help us."

Ms. Lensky stood up and put her foot firmly in the ruined cake. Then she lifted it.

"Ms. Lensky, I owe you an apology," said Gwen.

"You already wrote me one," said Ms. Lensky.

"This time I mean it," said Gwen. "Your heel print doesn't match the footprints we found outside in the snow with the tofu dogs." Gwen pointed to the heel print on the floor. "But Mr. Peacock's boot print does. It was Mr. Peacock in the kitchen."

"Mr. Peacock!" exclaimed Mr. Liu.

Gwen looked out at the lunchroom. Mr. Peacock was whispering in the principal's ear. Gwen narrowed her eyes.

"Let's wheel out the cake," said Gwen. "It's time for the real culprit to be exposed."

"What is she talking about?" asked Ms. Lensky.

"I think she's about to cook Mr. Peacock's goose," said Jill.

"Is this a joke?" asked the mayor.

"No," said Gwen. "There was a fire in the oven because it doesn't work right. Nothing works right in the cafeteria."

"Excuse me," said Mr. Peacock. "This girl is a trouble-maker. I have proof these two deliberately burned this cake as a prank."

"Gwen and Jill were never in trouble before the new cafeteria opened," said Mrs. Greaton.

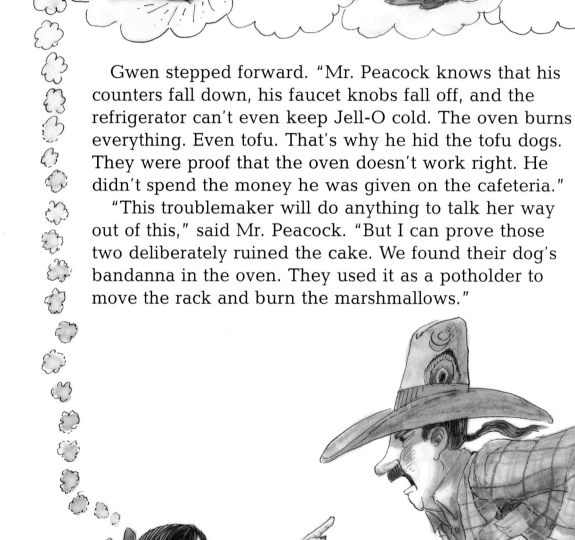

Gwen stepped forward. "Mr. Peacock knows that his counters fall down, his faucet knobs fall off, and the refrigerator can't even keep Jell-O cold. The oven burns everything. Even tofu. That's why he hid the tofu dogs. They were proof that the oven doesn't work right. He didn't spend the money he was given on the cafeteria."

"This troublemaker will do anything to talk her way out of this," said Mr. Peacock. "But I can prove those two deliberately ruined the cake. We found their dog's bandanna in the oven. They used it as a potholder to move the rack and burn the marshmallows."

SALAMI

"You found out Fletcher was Jill's dog from Jill's mom," said Gwen.

Jill's mom nodded.

"He wanted to blame us," Gwen continued, "so he could keep the money he should have spent on the cafeteria. He was quick. I noticed he didn't have *his* bandanna on after the cake burned. He planted it in the oven and took Fletcher's bandanna when we were all looking at the ruined cake. Here it is." Gwen pulled a red bandanna from Mr. Peacock's pocket. It had Fletcher's name on it.

Mr. Peacock flipped a carrot stick at Gwen's face and started to run. Fletcher leaped and caught the carrot. He spit it out. Cottontails chew crunchy carrots. Not Fletcher. Instead Fletcher grabbed Mr. Peacock's pant leg and held on.

CARROT STICK

(A FLETCHER COTTONTAIL CHEWING A CRUNCHY CARROT)

The mayor stood up to her full height. "Mr. Peacock, I'll see you pay back every penny you pocketed instead of buying first-class equipment."

"Thank you, Gwen," said Ms. Lensky. "You really saved my day. How can I repay you?"

"No more tofu dogs!" said Gwen and Jill in unison.

"To tell you the truth, I never liked them much myself," said Ms. Lensky.

The whole class cheered, and Fletcher's tail wagged faster than ever.